trat

or tran
anical,

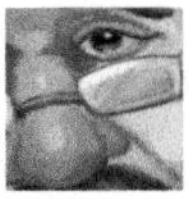

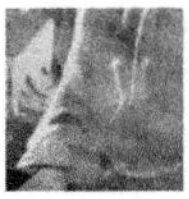

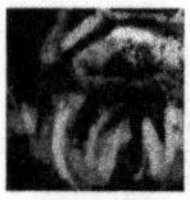

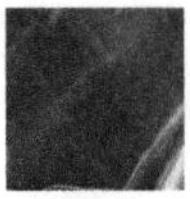

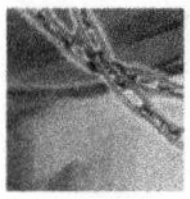

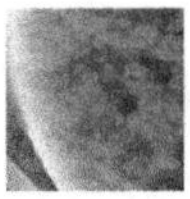

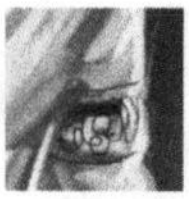

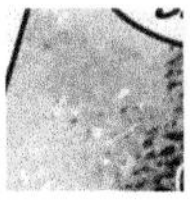

r's
AS!

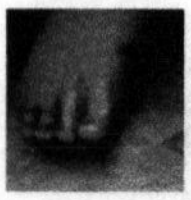

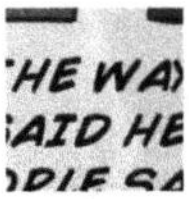

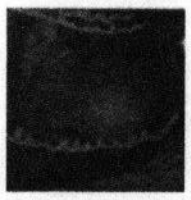

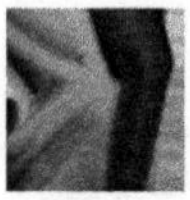

HAVE B
NDER...

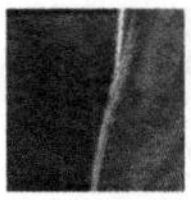

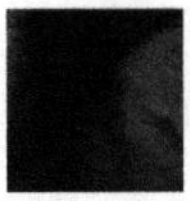

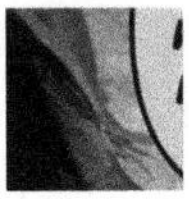

CHRI

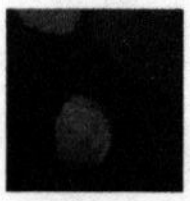

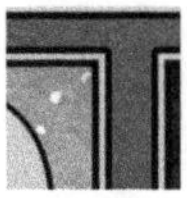

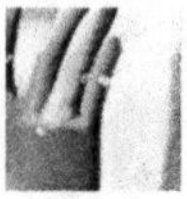

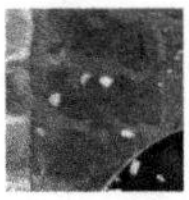

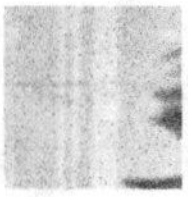

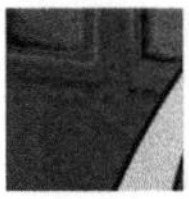

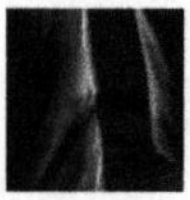

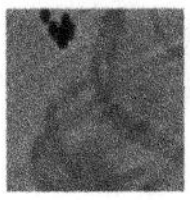

Printed in the USA
CPSIA information can be obtained
at www.ICGtesting.com
LVHW071130081223
766015LV00029B/129

9 789391 476236